P9-CMV-363

By Robert Kraus

For Parker

A GOLDEN BOOK • NEW YORK
Western Publishing Company, Inc., Racine, Wisconsin 53404

 Library of Congress Catalog Card Number: 92-73781 ISBN: 0-307-11566-6/ISBN: 0-307-65656-X (lib. bdg.) A MCMXCIII

I was walking along
when I saw a big sign.

It said:

I felt sad.
Spiders can't dance.
But I wanted to enter
the contest.

Just then my friends
Fly and Ladybug came along.
"Are you going
to the dance tonight, Spider?"
asked Ladybug.
"I'll save you a dance."

"No, I'm not going," I said.
"You see, I can't dance."

"Sure, you can," said Ladybug.
"Watch me.
One, two, three, kick!"

I tried to follow Ladybug.
But I have eight legs.
I didn't know which one
to kick first.

"Look," said Fly.
"I'm dancing cheek to cheek
with Ladybug."

I tried to follow Fly.
But I couldn't get my cheek
to touch Ladybug's cheek.

"I just can't dance,"
I said.
"Come to the dance anyway,"
said Ladybug.
"You can be a wallflower,"
said Fly.

"Thanks, but no thanks,"
I said.

Then I got an idea.

I would take dancing lessons.
I went downtown
to Madam LaZonga's dancing school.

“Can you teach me to dance?”
I asked Madam LaZonga.
“Oh, yes,” she said.
“In three easy lessons.”

First we tried ballroom dancing.
"Slide and glide,"
said Madam LaZonga.

I tried to slide.

I tried to glide.

But my legs got tangled up.

Then we tried ballet.
“On your toes,”
said Madam LaZonga.

But I have too many toes.
I couldn't stay on all of them
at the same time.

“Don’t worry,”
said Madam LaZonga.
“I know you can
shake, rattle, and roll.”

I could shake.
I could rattle.
But I couldn't roll.
My legs got in the way.
All eight of them!

"I'm sorry," said Madam LaZonga.
"You're my first failure."
"Thanks anyway," I said.

I went home
and took a shower.

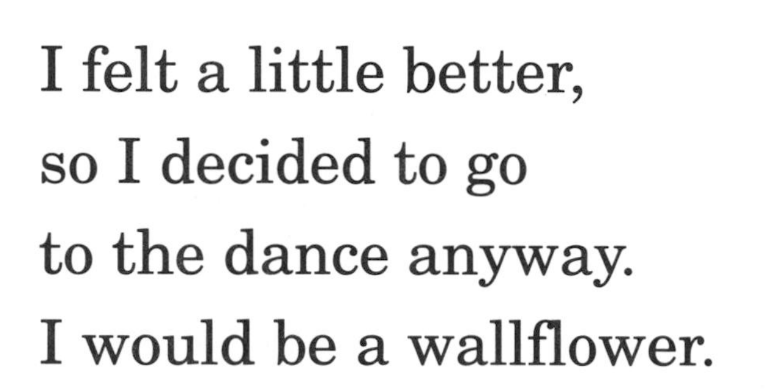

I felt a little better,
so I decided to go
to the dance anyway.
I would be a wallflower.

When I got to the school,
the Bug Band was swinging.
Every bug in the gym
was dancing.
The place was jumping.

The litterbugs were doing the jitterbug.
Fly was doing the cha-cha.
The bedbugs were doing
the bedbug hop.

The caterpillars were doing
the twist.
But where was Ladybug?

Then I saw Ladybug coming
into the gym.
She was carrying a bunch
of balloons.

Suddenly a gust of wind
blew through the door.
Ladybug went up, up, and away.
"Save me, save me!"
she cried.

Ladybug needed my help.
I jumped as high as I could.
I grabbed her foot
and pulled her down.

Then she let go of the balloons.
I jumped again and
pulled the balloons down.

But I landed on a banana peel!

Wh-o-o-o-ps!

"Wow!" said Fly.
"What do you call that dance?"
"Spider's Banana Split,"
I said.

“Dance, Spider, dance!”
cheered Ladybug.
So I did.
I jumped as high as I could . . .

and I landed on the banana peel again.
This time I slid right in front
of the judges.

“Spider is the winner
of the contest!”
said the judges.
“He’s got rhythm!”

Ladybug gave me a kiss.
Fly gave me a handshake.
I was very happy.

To celebrate, we all went
to the ice-cream store.
We had banana splits, of course.
It was my treat!